FOR William
J.S.

FOR Gorgeous George
J.C.

LITTLE TIGER PRESS
An imprint of Magi Publications
1 The Coda Centre, 189 Munster Road, London SW6 6AW
www.littletigerpress.com

First published in Great Britain 1999
This edition published 2007

A CIP catalogue record for this book is available from
the British Library

2 4 6 8 10 9 7 5 3 1

Smudge

by
Julie Sykes
illustrated by
Jane Chapman

LITTLE TIGER PRESS
London

Smudge was playing in the garden
with his friends, Nibble and Bounce.
The sun was shining and they were
having so much fun that they didn't
notice the big black cloud
drifting overhead.

PLOP!

"What was that?" asked Smudge, looking up.

SPLASH! SPLATTER!

Suddenly the sky went dark and large
raindrops began to fall.

"Oh, wriggling raindrops!" squeaked Smudge.

"That one got me on the nose!"

"It's only a summer shower," said Nibble.

"It won't last."

"Help! We're getting wet!"
cried Smudge. "I'm going indoors."
He raced towards the house,
but when he got there . . .

. . . the door was shut!

"Let me in," barked Smudge. But no one heard him, even when he howled and scratched.

"There must be another way in," thought Smudge. "Perhaps the window's open?"

The window *was* open –
but it was too high for
Smudge to reach.
Underneath it was
a stack of
flowerpots.

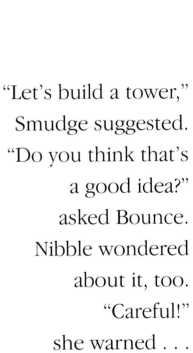

"Let's build a tower,"
Smudge suggested.
"Do you think that's
a good idea?"
asked Bounce.
Nibble wondered
about it, too.
"Careful!"
she warned . . .

. . . CRASH!

It was too late! Smudge and the flowerpots tumbled to the ground.

"That didn't work," said Smudge, picking himself up. "But I have a better idea!"

"Oh, no!" groaned Bounce.
"Not another one!"
"Let's go to your hutch,"
barked Smudge.
Bounce led the way across
the garden. Smudge followed
close behind.
"Wait for me!" panted Nibble.

"Come along, there's room for
everyone," cried Smudge.
Only . . .

. . . there wasn't!

"What now?" asked Nibble.

"I know," said Smudge.

"Follow me, everyone. This is
my best idea yet!"

Nibble and Bounce followed Smudge back
towards the house.

Smudge got there first.

"Oh, no!" cried Bounce. "I can't watch this."

"Easy," said Smudge, as he poked his
nose through the cat flap.

And it *was* easy until . . .

. . . he found he was stuck!
"I knew it!" said Bounce.
"Help me!" barked Smudge.
"*Now* what shall I do?"
"Stop wriggling and we'll
lend you a paw,"
squeaked Nibble.
Nibble and Bounce pushed
on Smudge's bottom.
They pushed and pushed and

PUSHED

until . . .

... *POP!*

Smudge shot
through the
cat flap and
landed,
nose down,
on the mat.

"Easy!" he cried,
shaking himself dry.

"Come along, Nibble,
your turn next."
But when Smudge
looked through the
cat flap he saw . . .

. . . the rain had stopped!
It was only a shower after all.
At the end of the garden, Nibble
and Bounce were playing together in
the sunshine.
"Wait!" cried Smudge. "I want to play too,
but . . .

". . . how am I going to get out again?"

Smudge looked around . . .

Then he had a *great* idea . . .